The Boy Who Cried Wolf

Retold by Elizabeth Adams

Illustrated by Daniel Howarth

Crabtree Publishing Company

www.crabtreebooks.com

Crabtree Publishing Company
www.crabtreebooks.com
1-800-387-7650

PMB 59051, 350 Fifth Ave.   616 Welland Ave.
59th Floor,   St. Catharines, ON
New York, NY 10118   L2M 5V6

Published by Crabtree Publishing in 2012

Series editor: Jackie Hamley
Editor: Kathy Middleton
Proofreader: Reagan Miller
Series advisor: Dr. Hilary Minns
Series designer: Peter Scoulding
**Production coordinator and
    Prepress technician:** Margaret Amy Salter
Print coordinator: Katherine Berti

Text © Franklin Watts 2009
Illustration © Daniel Howarth 2009

Printed in the USA/012019/VB20181217

First published in 2009
by Franklin Watts
(A division of Hachette
Children's Books)

**Library and Archives Canada
Cataloguing in Publication**

Adams, Elizabeth
     The boy who cried wolf [electronic resource] /
retold by Elizabeth Adams ; illustrated by Daniel
Howarth.

(Tadpoles: tales)
Electronic monograph.
Issued also in print format.
ISBN 978-1-4271-7929-6 (PDF).
--ISBN 978-1-4271-8044-5 (HTML)

     I. Howarth, Daniel II. Title. III. Series: Tadpoles
(St. Catharines, Ont. : Online). Tales

PZ8.2.A32Bo 2012   j398.22   C2012-
902487-2

**The Library of Congress
has cataloged the printed
edition as follows:**

Adams, Elizabeth.
 The boy who cried wolf / retold by Elizabeth
Adams ; illustrated by Daniel Howarth.
     p. cm. -- (Tadpoles: tales)
    ISBN 978-0-7787-7890-5 (reinforced library
binding : alk. paper) -- ISBN 978-0-7787-7902-5
(pbk. : alk. paper) -- ISBN 978-1-4271-7929-6
(electronic pdf : alk. paper) -- ISBN 978-1-4271-
8044-5 (electronic html : alk. paper)
     [1. Fables. 2. Folklore.] I. Howarth, Daniel, ill.
II. Aesop. III. Title.
    PZ8.2.A23Boy 2012
    398.2--dc23
    [E]
                                            2012015391

This kind of story is called a fable. It was written by a Greek author called Aesop over 2,500 years ago. Fables are stories that can teach something. Can you figure out what the lesson in this fable is?

Long ago, a boy
watched his sheep
near a village.

One day, he
was bored.

So he cried,
"Wolf! Wolf!"

The villagers
ran to help him.

7

When they got there,
the boy laughed.

"There is no wolf.
Tricked you!" he said.

Weeks later, the boy was bored again.

"Wolf! Wolf!"
he cried.

Again, the villagers
ran to help him.

13

When they got there,
the boy laughed
even more.

The villagers were annoyed.

The next day,
a wolf did come.

"Wolf! Wolf!"
cried the boy.

But this time nobody came

and the sheep
ran away.

So the boy went
home without his sheep.

Puzzle Time!

a
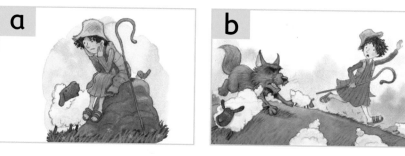

b

c

d

e

f

Put these pictures in the right order and tell the story!

annoyed

fed up

bored

angry

Which words describe the boy and which describe the villagers?

Turn the page for the answers!

Notes for adults

TADPOLES: TALES are structured for emergent readers. The books may also be used for read-alouds or shared reading with young children.

The Boy who cried Wolf is based on a classic fable by Aesop. Aesop's fables teach important principles about greed, patience, perseverance, and other character traits. Fables are a key type of literary text found in the Common Core State Standards.

IF YOU ARE READING THIS BOOK WITH A CHILD, HERE ARE A FEW SUGGESTIONS:

1. Make reading fun! Choose a time to read when you and the child are relaxed and have time to share the story.

2. Set a purpose for reading by explaining to the child that each of Aesop's fables teach a lesson. This information will help the reader understand the story and the features of the genre.

3. Encourage the child to reread the story and to retell it using his or her own words. Invite the child to use the illustrations as a guide.

4. Discuss the lesson of the story. Is the lesson important? Why or why not?

5. Give praise! Children learn best in a positive environment.

HERE ARE OTHER TITLES FROM TADPOLES: TALES FOR YOU TO ENJOY:

How the Camel got his Hump	978-0-7787-7888-2 RLB	978-0-7787-7900-1 PB
How the Elephant got its Trunk	978-0-7787-7891-2 RLB	978-0-7787-7903-2 PB
The Ant and the Grasshopper	978-0-7787-7889-9 RLB	978-0-7787-7901-8 PB
The Fox and the Crow	978-0-7787-7892-9 RLB	978-0-7787-7904-9 PB
The Lion and the Mouse	978-0-7787-7893-6 RLB	978-0-7787-7905-6 PB

VISIT WWW.CRABTREEBOOKS.COM FOR OTHER CRABTREE BOOKS.

Answers

Here is the correct order!
1. a 2. f 3. c 4. b 5. d 6. e

Words to describe the boy:
bored, fed up

Words to describe
the villagers:
angry, annoyed